The author and publishers would like to thank Dr. Philip Hammond
of the Sea Mammal Research Unit, University of St. Andrews, for his help.

Published by BridgeWater Paperback, an imprint and trademark of
Troll Communications L.L.C.

Published in hardcover in the United States and Canada by BridgeWater Books.

Arctic Song was edited, designed, and produced
and first published in the UK by Frances Lincoln Limited,
4 Torriano Mews, Torriano Avenue, London NW5 2RZ.
Reprinted by arrangement with Frances Lincoln Limited.

Printed in the United States of America.

10 9 8 7 6 5 4 3 2 1

Library of Congress Cataloging-in-Publication Data

Moss, Miriam.
Arctic song / Miriam Moss ; illustrated by Adrienne Kennaway.
p.   cm.
Summary: Bewitched by the raven's description of whalesong, two
polar bear cubs go in search of the whales, encountering caribou,
a walrus, and other animals on the way. Includes a factual page
about life in the Arctic.
ISBN 0-8167-6069-1 (lib. bdg.)   ISBN 0-8167-6519-7 (pbk.)
[1. Polar bear—Fiction. 2. Bears—Fiction. 3. Whales—Fiction.
4. Zoology—Arctic regions—Fiction.] I. Kennaway, Adrienne, ill.
II. Title.
PZ7.M8535Ar   1999
[E]—dc21   98-46372

ARCTIC SONG

MIRIAM MOSS

Illustrated by

ADRIENNE KENNAWAY

Troll
BridgeWater Paperback

There is a land of frozen darkness,
lost in ice and snow.
Every year, for a short time,
the sun visits
and the land of midnight
becomes the land of the midnight sun.

One morning, a mother polar bear
breaks through the snow roof of her den.
Her cubs follow,
stretching and blinking in the light.

The mother sniffs the air,
rolls over and over in the powdery snow,
and slides down the hill on her back.

The cubs pounce and play,
then skid down to the mint-green sea
to dabble their paws
and scratch designs on ice.

An inky raven looks for trouble.
He spies the cubs and flaps down.
With flashing feathers
and beady eye,
he weaves mischievous stories
about the magic
of whalesong.

The cubs are bewitched.

Sensing danger,
their mother turns,
arrows her wedge-shaped head,
and runs hissing, shooing the raven off.

Too late.
The cubs are curious.
"When can we hear whalesong, Mother?"
"When you are older," she says.
"Singing whales live far away. Too far."

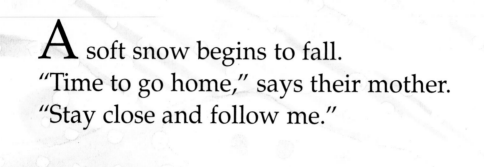

A soft snow begins to fall.
"Time to go home," says their mother.
"Stay close and follow me."

But the cubs hang back
until their mother
disappears into the haze.

Then they scamper off
to search for whalesong.

The cubs race through the snow
until small rocks and stones
break the whiteness.

The sun outlines a herd of caribou
tramping northward
in raggedy lines.
The last caribou chips at the snow crust
with her hoof.
"Where can we hear whalesong?"
"I do not know," says the caribou.

With dark mountains behind them
and snow geese overhead,
the cubs pad on.
Before them, a giant rock
turns into a great bearded musk ox.
The wind lifts and blows its shaggy hair
like curtains.
"Where can we hear whalesong?"
"I do not know," says the musk ox.

The cubs dance in buzzing meadows
threaded with silver streams
and carpeted with flowers.
Then, yawning,
they roll on beds of moss
and listen
to the Arctic loon's haunting cry.

A friendly fox trips by.
"Where can we hear whalesong?"
"At the sea," the fox replies.
"Go that way." She points. "It's not far."

The cubs splash through ice pools.
At the jagged ocean edge,
they watch monstrous icebergs,
shaped like castles,
drip in the midnight sun.

A walrus lounges on floating flat ice.
"Where can we hear whalesong?"
"Walrus song sounds better," he says. "Listen."
On the stony bottom of the shallow sea,
he plays his drumbeat song.
"Thank you," say the cubs,
"but we want to hear whalesong, too."

The sun's reflection shivers and scatters
as the cubs slide into the water.

Nearby, a narwhal points its spiraled tusk
at the clouds.
"Can you sing whalesong?" call the cubs.
"Dive deeper, dive deeper," says the narwhal.

With ivory coats smooth as silk,
the cubs plunge deep
into an underwater world
lit by the silvery flash of fish.

Above them,
a bowhead whale shoulders through the water,
her calf alongside,
her long, curved smile full of stiffly fringed hair.
She rises to let out a deep, deep blow, then dives
and starts to sing
whalesong,
her song,
a mother singing to her young.

"Time to go home," the song sings,
"before winter comes and darkness falls."

The cubs listen, spellbound.
For inside the song,
they hear their mother calling,
see her searching,
feel her waiting.

The cubs turn
and swim homeward,
shoulder to shoulder.

They climb onto land,
their coats running heavily
with jade-green droplets.

A stormy sky threatens.
A bitter wind bites deep.
Loose-limbed, they run across the ice,
snow flying from coats and paws.

At dusk, they reach their den.
"Mother," they shout, "we heard whalesong!"
A paw appears, then a head.

Seeing them, their mother's eyes light up.
Darkness falls,
and the snow shuffles softly again
over the roof of the warm den.

About the Arctic

The Arctic is an area of cold seas and cold lands surrounding the North Pole. During the Arctic winter, the sun does not rise over much of the region. Light comes from the moon and stars, reflecting off ice and snow. In summer, the sun is above the horizon for long periods, but the Arctic is rarely warm. There are some little trees. The plants are all small and slow-growing, and many have brilliantly colored flowers.

There are few land animals in the Arctic. The shaggy *musk ox* is smaller than an ordinary cow, but its coat is long and thick. Smaller still is the *caribou* (also known as a reindeer). *Polar bears*, by contrast, are very big and strong. They are powerful swimmers, at home both on land and in the sea. A layer of fat beneath the skin helps keep them warm in the icy waters. Polar bear mothers are devoted to their cubs, playing with them and protecting them from harm. When food is scarce, the mother is careful to divide it so that each cub gets its fair share.

An *Arctic fox* is about one third as long as a polar bear from nose to tail, but the bear is almost a hundred times heavier. There are two types of Arctic fox: one has a white winter coat and a brown summer coat, and the other changes from pale winter gray to darker gray in summer.

Few birds spend all year in the Arctic, but huge numbers fly north in the summer months to enjoy the long daylight hours, returning south when their young are able to fly with them.

Arctic waters are home to *walrus, seals, narwhals* and other whales, fish, and many smaller creatures. The whale whose songs are most familiar to humans through television and sound recordings is the humpback whale, but the *bowhead whale* has its own voice. Bowhead whales live only in the colder waters and rarely travel far from the ice. They make various noises, among them a loud "Hmmmm," sometimes rising, sometimes falling, through the northern seas.